THE WORLD'S GREATEST ATHLETE

Walt Disney Productions'

THE WORLD'S GREATEST ATHLETE

GERALD GARDNER and DEE CARUSO

**Illustrated with pictures
from the movie**

SCHOLASTIC BOOK SERVICES
New York Toronto London Auckland Sydney Tokyo

Copyright © 1973 by Walt Disney Productions. All rights
reserved. Published by Scholastic Book Services, a divi-
sion of Scholastic Magazines, Inc.

2nd printing . . . . May 1973
Printed in the U.S.A.

CAST

Jan-Michael Vincent
Nanu

Tim Conway
Milo Jackson

John Amos
Sam Archer

Roscoe Lee Browne
Gazenga

Billy De Wolfe
Dean Lacey

Dayle Haddon
Jane Douglas

Nancy Walker
Mrs. Peterson

Danny Goldman
Leopold Lacey

G.T.
Harri

Sam Archer,
Merrivale College
coach

Milo Jackson,
Archer's assistant

Nanu,
wonder athlete Archer
and Jackson find in
Africa and bring back
to Merrivale

Gazenga,
African witch doctor
who follows his godson
Nanu to America

Jane Douglas,
Nanu's lovely tutor in
America

(Left) Dean Lacey,

(Right) His son,
Leopold

Mrs. Peterson,
Nanu's nearsighted
landlady

Harri,
Nanu's pet tiger

CHAPTER ONE

What can you say about a coach who does nothing but lose?

A coach is expected to win. That's what a coach *does*. If you're a writer you write. If you're a plumber you plumb. And if you're a coach you win.

And I did nothing but lose.

Since Merrivale was a small college, I coached all the teams. And this gave me the opportunity to lose games in a wide variety of sports.

I lost games in football.

I lost games in baseball.

I lost games in basketball.

I lost track meets.

In fact, if the truth be known, I was one of the all-time great losers.

Back in '62 I was starting fullback at Michigan State when we went to the Rose Bowl.

I broke my ankle running onto the field.

Mind you, it didn't make me hate sports. I *love* sports.

I just hate losing.

And I tried. I really did.

In those locker-room sessions with the boys, I poured my heart out to them. I was sincere. I was confident...

"Fellas," I said, tossing a football and eyeing my football squad. "Fellas — football is my life...

"What are you doing out there?" I said. "You can take 'em. But you've got to *think*. You've got to use your *head*. You've got to be *alert*. Now go out there and win!"

And the boys rushed out the door.

"No, fellas, that's the shower!"

Or my baseball team.

We're in the dugout between innings.

"Fellas," I say, tossing a baseball for effect. "Fellas, baseball is my life. And I tell you we can beat these guys. But you've got to be *alert*. You've got to keep your eyes *open*. You've got to play *heads-up ball*. Now let's go!"

And my boys go rushing out of the dugout, trip over the bats, and go flying.

Or in the locker room with the basketball team.

"Fellas," I said, tossing a basketball. "Basketball is my life. What are you doing to me? You're missing rebounds — you're missing foul shots — but most of all, you're not playing to *win*! And believe me, fellas, if we pull together, we can win!"

The boys went rushing for the door.

"Fellas — the game's over. I mean *next* week..."

"If we pull together, we can win!" Merrivale Coach Sam Archer is confident, but the team's not so sure.

CHAPTER TWO

But all bad things must come to an end. And so finally did the semester.

It ended with the kind of humiliation that my assistant Milo and I had become accustomed to.

Broxton was beating Merrivale 46 to three.

With a few seconds to play, Gronsky did a handoff, and handed off to one of the Broxton linemen who had broken through our defense.

After the Broxton boy overcame his surprise, he ran for a touchdown.

53 to three.

Well, you can't win 'em all.

The boys limped off the field. Even the school band limped off the field. It was the last game of a degrading season.

As Milo and I headed for the locker

Assistant Coach Milo Jackson crosses his fingers for luck, but Archer seems sceptical.

room, we were interrupted by *him*.

Him is Dean Lacey. There's a lot of conflicting opinion about Dean Lacey. Some people think he's petty and malicious. Others feel just the opposite — that he's malicious and petty.

Dean Lacey had stamped across from his field box and he didn't look happy. Neither did his son Leopold, the perennial graduate student and carbon copy of his father.

"In all my years at Merrivale," said Lacey, "I have never seen a season like this."

"Never like this," said Leopold.

"We lost ten football games, twenty-six basketball games, thirty-two baseball games," said the Dean.

"Five of them were practice games," said Leopold.

A cheerleader limped by.

"We lost every track meet we entered," said Lacey. "Only our Ping Pong team broke even."

"That was because they came down with measles and canceled the schedule," said Leopold.

A tuba player from the marching band limped by.

"I'll tell you this, Archer," growled the Dean. "I don't see how the college could survive another season like this one."

Leopold put the knife in just below the third rib.

"Of course, Father," he purred, "the coach *does* have a contract for next year."

That's when pride took hold of me. I pulled a document from my pocket.

"Don't let my contract worry you," I snapped. "I'm tearing it up."

I shredded the paper, tossed it to the

Archer tells Dean Lacey what he can do with his contract.
Leopold, Lacey's obnoxious son, looks on with obvious
satisfaction.

ground, and walked off the field. It was
my finest moment.

Milo came scurrying after me.

"Where are you going, Coach?" asked
Milo. "The locker room is the other
way."

"I want to get as far away from this
campus as possible," I said.

Milo stopped short.

"Wait a minute," he said. "I'm going
to resign too."

"You already did," I said. "That was
your contract."

CHAPTER THREE

There's a fable about a boy who found a lion limping through the jungle, a thorn in his foot. He removed the thorn and sent the beast on his way. Years later the lion came charging through the village where the boy lived. He saw the boy and stopped. Then, after a moment's pause, he devoured the boy.

Lions don't remember things like that.

If there's any useful moral to that story, it's that the jungle helps you forget. Even if you're a lion. So why not if you're a coach?

A week after the traumatic incident on the playing fields of Merrivale, Milo and I were part of a safari threading our way through a game preserve in Zambia.

Milo wasn't too happy about the trip. "Getting away is one thing," he mumbled, "but Africa! There are wild animals around here!"

Archer and Milo go to Africa for a vacation. Here they are, walking through a game preserve in Zambia.

"I felt a need to get back to my roots," I said.

"Then why didn't we go to Cleveland?" said Milo.

"I mean my *real* roots," I said. "My great grandparents came from this part of Africa. Besides, I was getting fed up with that whole college scene. I couldn't stand to lose another game."

"It wasn't your fault, Coach," said Milo. "The school won't spend any money on athletics."

But Milo's attempts to salve my feelings didn't help. I explained for the umpteenth time that I was a failure as a coach. My teams had lost consistently in every imaginable sport.

"Well, winning isn't everything," said Milo.

"It is if you're a coach."

Suddenly one of the lady tourists started shouting and pointing across the veldt.

"Look at that!" she cried.

She was pointing at one of the most graceful sights I had ever seen. It was a gazelle, racing across the horizon.

"That's a gazelle," I told Milo, "the fastest animal in the jungle."

(Right) Nanu, the world's greatest athlete, runs far ahead of a gazelle he is racing.
(Below) Archer, Milo, and chief bearer Morumba watch Nanu racing through the woods.

"Not as fast as Nanu," said the chief bearer.

"What's a nanu?" asked Milo.

Before the chief bearer could answer, the lady tourist started screaming again.

"*Look!*" she shouted.

And off on the horizon, I saw it.

A boy streaking along, gaining on the gazelle, running abreast of it, and then, would you believe? *passing* it!

"Nanu!" said the bearer with satisfaction.

Now, I had a straight B average at Michigan State. I don't lay claim to any great intellectual gifts. But I don't have to have a cathedral fall on me to see the obvious.

That boy was the greatest natural athlete I had ever seen.

I had to see more of him.

An hour later, Milo and I and chief bearer Morumba were squatting in a ditch watching the boy through our binoculars.

Nanu was racing through the woods, dodging in and out of the trees, showing incredible agility.

Something in my mind clicked into

place like an automatic slide projector, and all I could see was the boy dodging Broxton tacklers on the Merrivale gridiron.

Thirty minutes later we had traded the ditch for a tree trunk, and I was peering out at the boy again.

This time he was on the branch of a date nut tree overhanging the river. He was tossing the large round fruit to children on the opposite shore, where one of the kids was holding a small wicker basket. The fruit was traveling in a smooth, curving trajectory, right into the basket.

And in my mind's eye was Nanu, in the Merrivale gymnasium, sinking 50-foot baskets.

An hour later we lay in the weeds watching Nanu hurl a spear at a narrow tree, 60 feet away.

Well, if he could hit that tree with a spear at 60 feet, why couldn't he hit the plate with a baseball at the same distance?

"Milo, congratulate me," I said. "I just made the Rose Bowl."

CHAPTER FOUR

"Talk about your Jim Thorpe — this is the most remarkable all-round athlete in the world. With the right kind of coaching, he could be a marvel in any sport he tried."

Those were my thoughts as I shinnied up a 200-foot-high date palm tree like an overeager telephone lineman.

Nanu, you see, was standing on the top branch of said tree, his hands on his hips, like an ad for *Tarzan's Revenge*, looking out over the expanse of his jungle home.

Finally I pulled myself up on the branch, stood there panting and puffing and holding on for dear life. I put on a cordial face and began.

"Hi. I wonder if I might — "

He gave me a look like a frightened fawn, grabbed a vine, and swung off.

Well, faint heart ne'er won decathlon

winner. I grabbed another vine and swung after him.

The vine carried me to the branch of another tree where I landed next to Nanu. The boy stood looking at me warily.

I tried again.

"Hello there. I just arrived from —"

He was off. He grabbed another vine and swung effortlessly to another tree.

In for a penny, in for a pound. I grabbed another vine and swung after him. Again, I landed heavily on a branch beside him. But this time, the branch extended far out over the river.

"Excuse me," I said. "Do you have a moment —"

The boy had dived into the river.

Trying to persuade him to go to America, Archer pursues Nanu up into a tree.

It was a clean, graceful dive, but at the moment I was not considering his Olympic potential. I stripped off my jacket and pith helmet, hung them on a jutting limb, and leaped, feet first, into the muddy river.

I came up near the boy.

"You have the makings — " I began.

But he was off again, swimming strongly to shore. I swam after him and pulled myself up on the sandy beach. I looked up and there was Nanu, seated on a boulder, staring down at me as though I had just crawled out from under a rock. He was holding a handful of nuts.

Archer realizes he will have to follow Nanu into the river if he wants to talk with him.

"I want . . . to take you . . . back to America with me," I gasped.

Then I heard the first words spoken by this superathlete.

"Nanu never leave jungle," he said.

"Now listen," I said, pulling myself to my feet and leaning heavily on a large gray boulder. "You have tremendous talent. You could win at any sport you tried."

"Why?" said Nanu.

"Why what?"

"Why win?"

"Why win?? Well, to be Number *One*. To be the *best*. To come in *first*."

"Why be first?"

Archer swims to shore where Nanu tells him, "Nanu never leave jungle."

Well, I'd never heard such un-American talk in my life. I guess my jaw went slack as I stared at this beautiful primitive, cracking walnuts in his fist. I tried again.

"Listen. If you come back with me, I could make you the world's greatest athlete. You could be *famous*. You could make a *fortune*. Then, after a few years, you could do anything you want."

"Nanu doing that now," said the boy.

And he ran off, leaving me wet, bothered, and bewildered.

I slammed my fist down on the boulder. It was an act of impotent fury. It was also a mistake.

The boulder started to rise. And to roar. The big gray boulder was a rhino.

Archer has just realized what he's sitting on.

CHAPTER FIVE

Next day the safari was busier than a cat with two mice. We were out on the hunt. The members of the safari were carrying rifles and were all moving cautiously through the jungle. Ahead of us went the bearers, beating the bushes to flush the wild game.

I had no heart for it. My wild game was out there in the jungle with my career in his pocket.

"It's what every coach dreams about," I told Milo. "The perfect athlete. But how do I get him out of a coconut tree and into a locker room?"

"What's his problem, coach?"

"The kid has no desire to *compete*," I explained. "He doesn't want to win. He's happy where he is."

I had spoken to Morumba, the chief bearer, and learned something of the boy's background. The jungle was the only world he knew. His parents were missionaries who had died when he was a baby, so the locals had raised him.

"There's got to be a way of getting him out," I said. "Got to be a way."

Just then four bearers passed, carrying an empty bamboo cage that was used for carrying wild beasts.

The moment I saw the cage, I stared.

"Coach — you can't *do* that!"

"You're right" I agreed. "We'd never get it on the plane."

Just then, Morumba came running up, looking agitated.

"Bwana — where is your rifle? Very dangerous to be on hunt without rifle."

"I left it back in the tent," I said.

"Morumba send gun bearer for it."

And with that he called to a nearby bearer and told him, in Swahili, to get the bwana's rifle.

The bearer trotted off, followed by a second man who ran in his wake.

"Does it take two gunbearers to bring back one gun?" I asked.

"No, Bwana," said Morumba. He pointed to the second man. "That man once save other man's life. Tribal law say, when you save a man's life, you become responsible for him — must go wherever *he* goes."

Suddenly it hit me.

"Wait a minute," I said. "You mean if someone saves a man's life, he has to follow him everywhere?"

"Yes, Bwana."

"Milo," I said, "we won't need the cage."

A little later, Milo and I were walking through a patch of swampy land. We stopped in a dry spot and I surveyed the general area.

"You sure there's quicksand around here, Milo?"

"Yeah, it's all around us, Coach."

"Okay. Now here's how we get the boy to save my life." I pointed to the branch of a nearby tree. "You'll be up in the tree watching the trail. When you see him, you give me the signal and I'll step into the quicksand."

Milo seemed to be getting shorter.

"He should be in sight any minute, so make sure you have it right."

Milo is definitely getting shorter.

"You're in the tree, you spot Nanu on

29

Milo gets shorter as Archer surveys the general situation.

Better late than never! But Milo is pretty disgusted with Archer's delayed reaction.

the path, you give me the signal."

Milo was gesturing to me now.

"Just listen," I said. "You're in the tree, he's on the path, I'm in the quicksand."

Then I realized.

Milo was sinking in quicksand.

"No, no, no," I said. "*I'm* in the quicksand and *you're* in the tree. Is that so hard to remember?"

I could see the quicksand wouldn't work.

"Let me think," I said as we plodded back to the encampment. "That kid has got to save my life before the plane leaves — "

Milo, as usual, was thinking only of himself.

"Boy, that quicksand is dangerous. I might have been killed. I was really dying — "

That was the idea I needed.

Twenty minutes later the stage was set.

I was lying on my cot, wrapped in blankets. My face was flushed, which wasn't hard to manage in a stuffy jungle tent. When Milo and Nanu burst in, I was ready.

Making slits of my eyes, I could see Nanu looking down at me with concern.

"White man look very sick," he said.

"The coach is in a coma," said Milo.

Then he produced the aspirin bottle.

"You've got to take this bottle to the village of Mombassa. It's the only thing that will save the coach's life."

But the kid had other ideas.

"Jungle medicine better," he said. "Nanu take coach to his godfather — Gazenga, the witch doctor."

And before I could say Joe Namath, the boy had thrown off my blankets, picked me up in his arms, hoisted me onto his shoulders in a fireman's carry, and trotted out of the tent.

"Coach need Gazenga!" said Nanu.

"Not Gazenga, Mombassa!" shouted Milo.

But by then the kid was racing through the jungle, with Milo in hot pursuit.

That was the most precarious trip of my life. The kid ran through foliage where the vines and leaves did unpleasant things to my face.

Then he threaded his way along a mountain path, where the sight of a

1,000-foot drop did unpleasant things to my stomach.

Finally, he arrived at his destination, a mountain cave whose entrance was guarded by two armed men. We plunged inside.

The cave was bathed in shadows. The dank walls were covered with an assortment of hideous-looking death masks, and a torch or two for illumination.

Nanu deposited me on the ground, and from that vantage point I looked up at one of the most chilling sights I've ever seen.

Bestriding my body like a black colossus was a witch doctor.

Gazenga.

I guess anything would have looked a little frightening from that angle. But with his huge, grotesque mask, the bone bracelets that circled his neck and wrist, and the ceremonial paint that striped his tall, muscular body, Gazenga looked especially fearful.

"White man need help," said Nanu. "Very sick."

By now Milo had come panting into the cave, and stood near the entrance looking apprehensive.

The witch doctor held up his hand.

"First Gazenga must administer jungle justice," he said.

He gestured toward two men who were cowering in the rear of the cave.

"One of these men is guilty of a crime," he said. "I will determine the guilty man."

With that, he produced a bowl of fluid from a shelf.

"They will both drink this poison. Innocent man will live — guilty man will die."

He handed the bowl first to one man, then to the other. Each took a sip of the liquid. We all stared at the two men, wondering which would fall.

After a long moment, one of the men grabbed his throat and pitched forward. Then the other man grabbed his throat and fell forward.

"Either they're both guilty, or he used too much poison," said Milo.

I suddenly felt a lot better.

"I just need a good night's sleep," I said and started to get up.

"Stay, man of little faith!" boomed Gazenga. "I can cure you."

The witch doctor gestured toward the

Witch doctor Gazenga offers a healing potion, but Archer is dubious.

cave entrance and the sound of jungle drums began.

"Now to your medicine," he said.

The witch doctor squatted on the floor by a smouldering cauldron and started adding ingredients.

"What are you putting in there?" I said.

Gazenga called off the items as he dropped them in.

"Zebra blood...cobra milk...rhinoceros marrow...lizard's tongue...the entrails of a goat...the skin of a hibernating toad..."

"I really feel much better," I said.

But by now Gazenga was chanting some weird incantation and nothing would satisfy him short of my drinking that bilious concoction.

He filled a bowl with the mixture and bent over me, urging the medicine down my unwilling throat.

"How is it?" asked Milo.

"Little too much lizard's tongue."

Now I felt *really* sick.

I started to moan a bit, as the zebra blood and rhinocerous marrow went coursing down my gullet.

"Him still sick," said Nanu, who was watching with a childlike innocence.

I figured here was my chance to turn lemon into lemonade.

"The medicine!" I moaned. "I need the medicine from the village!"

And Milo, bless him, produced the aspirin bottle and handed it to the boy. Nanu darted a sheepish look at his godfather and raced out of the cave.

I waited.

It was quite a wait, and Gazenga wouldn't give up on curing me himself.

First he opened my shirt and started

painting a series of multicolored stripes on my chest.

"What does this do?" I said.

"It lets people know you're one of my patients."

When that didn't work, he trussed me up and suspended me from the ceiling by my ankles.

"Why are you doing this?" I asked.

"This is to make the blood rush to your head," said Gazenga.

"It's working," I said.

By the time Nanu returned from the medical settlement with a full bottle of aspirin, Gazenga had me covered with a handsome assortment of feathers.

"Just in time," I said. "I was ready to fly south."

Nanu handed the aspirin bottle to Milo and he quickly fed me two of them with some water.

My expression changed dramatically from pain to relief. I stood up.

"*I'm cured!*" I shouted. "*I feel wonderful!*"

"What a miraculous recovery," said Milo.

"You saved my life," I said to Nanu. "Boy, did you save my life."

Then I turned to Milo. "This boy saved my life," I said. "He definitely saved my life."

I turned to Gazenga and shook his hand.

"Good-bye, Gazenga."

Archer looks wistful wearing the witch doctor's feathers.

While Archer writhes on the ground in simulated pain, everyone else debates the value of aspirin as a remedy.

Then I shook hands with the assistant chief. "Good-bye, sir."

Then I shook Nanu's hand.

"And good-bye to you, the *boy who saved my life*."

And I started out of the cave.

"Wait!" said Gazenga.

I knew he would.

"Nanu," said the witch doctor softly. "You know our tribal law. You must go with him."

The boy looked stunned.

"When you save a man's life," continued Gazenga, "you must go with him wherever he goes."

I played it to the hilt.

"Wait a minute," I snapped. "You mean I've got to take this kid with me? No chance."

"What must be, must be," said Gazenga.

"But what am I gonna *do* with him?"

"He could play foot — " began Milo.

I kicked him and he stopped.

"I don't want a kid hanging around my neck," I said.

"It is tribal law," said Gazenga with finality.

"Now let me get this straight," I said.

Gazenga explains to his assistant that since Nanu has saved Archer's life by bringing him aspirin, Nanu must, by tribal law, follow Archer to the United States.

"You mean to tell me that your ancient tribal law demands that this poor boy be uprooted from his home and travel thousands of miles to some strange, far-away land?"

"That is so."

I turned to the kid.

"The plane leaves at noon. Be on it."

CHAPTER SIX

I had done it.

I had found the most remarkable physical specimen in the world, and in another few days I would have him safely ensconced in Merrivale College, Home of the Loser.

These pleasant thoughts were circulating through my brain as the little prop-driven, trimotor plane carrying our safari lifted into the Zambian air, leaving a swirl of dust and assorted natives and jungle beasts behind it.

It was kind of touching. They had come to see the boy off. There was Gazenga looking intense and telling me I had better take good care of him or else. There were four zebras and a chimpanzee. It looked like the Dean at a pajama party.

I settled back into my seat, with Milo

beside me. My brain started perking.

"Now, here's what we have to do soon as we get back," I said. "Get this down..."

Milo produced a pad and pencil.

"It may be a little tricky. First we'll have to enroll him at Merrivale — work out a curriculum — get him a tutor — buy him some clothes — teach him the fundamentals of sports. Do you have all that?"

"All but the last part," said Milo.

"What do you mean the last part?"

"The part after 'It may be a little tricky,' " said Milo.

"Did you have any trouble getting the kid on board?" I asked.

"Well, he was a little unhappy about leaving his tiger behind."

"Well, that's only natural," I said. "I hope you explained that we can't very well have a tiger roaming around a college campus."

"Oh sure."

"Good."

"Now," said Milo, "somebody ought to explain it to the tiger."

Trouble.

"Where's the kid?" I said.

"In the baggage compartment."

I headed for the rear of the plane and stepped behind the partition into the baggage area. There they were.

Nanu and friend. A 400-pound snaggle-toothed tiger.

"Harri worried," said Nanu. "Not like plane."

"Tell him not to worry," I said. "No sense *everybody* worrying."

On the drive from the Merrivale Airport to the boardinghouse, Milo started to turn waspish. Maybe it was having that tiger in the back seat.

"We're gonna have to put him in a zoo, you know," snapped Milo. "There's no place for wild animals at a college.

"Harri not go into zoo," said the kid. "Nanu like to be around animals. Besides, tiger very smart."

"Maybe we should put *you* in the zoo and enroll the tiger," said Milo.

The kid sulked. The tiger growled.

"I won't sleep a wink with that animal in the house," said Milo.

"It could be worse," I said. "His best friend could have been an elephant."

We pulled up to the boardinghouse that I'd called home during the year I'd been presiding over the defeats of the Merrivale squads.

"You know Mrs. Peterson won't allow the tiger in the house," said Milo. "No way."

"With *her* eyes, maybe she won't see him," I said. "You know she can't see past the end of her nose."

We pulled up close to the front door and Nanu and I, holding the tiger upright between us, moved him toward the entrance. We had him in an overcoat and a ten-gallon hat. Which made him look to the naked eye like a tiger in an overcoat and a ten-gallon hat.

But Mrs. Peterson's weren't normal eyes. As we approached the front door, Mrs. Peterson was watering her garden. Milo spun her around the other way, flashed some snapshots of our trip, and told her that we had brought a couple of friends from Zambia.

Mrs. Peterson bent an astigmatic eye on the tiger, whom Nanu and I were supporting between us.

"You know my rules about drinking," she said.

Mrs. Petersen, the landlady, can't see that it is the tail of Harri, the tiger, she holds, not her garden hose.

Fifteen minutes later, Nanu was safely bedded down in a spare bedroom, and Milo and I were reviewing our plan of attack for the following day.

"Tomorrow I enroll the kid at Merrivale," I said. "I'll have to get him in as a sophomore so he can play on the varsity."

"But will they buy him as an exchange student from Zambia University?" said Milo.

"Why shouldn't they?"

"Well, he doesn't look the part," said Milo.

"Have you seen any exchange students from Zambia University?"

"No," said Milo.

"That's what they look like," I said. "Come on. Let's see what he's up to."

That's when I got my laugh of the day.

We walked into the bedroom and found the kid sitting on the bed, holding a straw voodoo doll in his hand, staring at it intently.

"What are you doing?" I asked.

"Nanu make voodoo doll," said the kid. "Gazenga taught Nanu mysteries of black magic."

"May I see it?"

He handed me the doll and I gave it the once-over. It was a simple straw doll about six inches long. And now I noticed that it bore a resemblance to Milo.

"Why Milo?" I asked.

"Milo not like Nanu's friend Harri. Anyone not like Nanu's friend, not like Nanu."

I tried to suppress a smile. Imagine

the kid thinking that a silly little voo-doo doll could actually hurt somebody. But he believed it all right. There were even a number of long pins on the bed.

"Now listen, Nanu," I said as patient-ly as I could. "You're in a civilized country now. You're going to have to put all those ridiculous superstitions behind you. It's just plain silly to think you can hurt someone by sticking pins in a doll."

I took a long pin from the bed and jabbed into the front of the doll.

Behind me, Milo grabbed his chest.

"I mean, that's crazy."

I jabbed a second pin lower into the doll and Milo grabbed his leg.

"This is just straw," I said and twist-ed the doll's arm. Milo's arm flew upward.

"Now I'm telling you, this mumbo-jumbo has to *stop — end — finish!*"

I hit the doll on the bedside table for emphasis. Behind me, Milo was slam-ming his head on the dresser.

"For thousands of years mankind has been turning from the ways of witch-craft and ignorance to the ways of science and knowledge — "

As I reasoned with the kid, I nervously tossed the doll up and down. Behind me, Milo was doing backflips.

"Now, we've got a busy day tomorrow. So let's not hear any more about dolls."

I tossed the doll over my shoulder and out the open window. Behind me, Milo was catapulted out the other window.

"Now, I want you and Milo to shake hands and be friends. Okay?"

I turned around and looked for my assistant.

"Now where did he go?" I said. "He's never around when you want him."

As Archer tosses Nanu's voodoo doll, made in the image of Milo, into the air, Milo suddenly does backflips.

CHAPTER SEVEN

The first hurdle was Mr. Peabody, our
fussy little registrar.

Leaving Milo and Nanu out in the
waiting room, I breezed into Peabody's
private office, nodded at Miss Bellows
who was busy at the filing cabinet, and
approached Peabody's neatly organized
desk.

"Peabody!" I said with a show of
surprise. "Are you still here?"

"Why yes," said Peabody. "What do
you mean?"

"Well," I said, sitting down on a
corner of his desk and moving his in-
basket, "you know we've had a heavy
turnover in registrars."

"No, I didn't know that," said Peabody, moving his in-basket back in
place.

"Six in three years," I said, and
moved his pencil jar.

"That many," said Peabody, and moved the pencil jar back.

"I guess you know what happened to Henderson, your immediate predecessor."

"No, I always wondered."

I leaned over and adjusted the knot of Peabody's tie.

"Henderson turned down a fullback because he didn't have the grades."

"Well, that's only right," said the registrar.

"The day the kid made All-America, Henderson went on unemployment."

Peabody grimaced. "Is it all right to turn down a shortstop?"

"*I* wouldn't," I said.

Peabody started adjusting the position of his stapler and began blinking rapidly.

"But listen," I said, "I'm not going to tell you how to run your office."

Miss Bellows looked out the office door.

"The next applicant is still waiting, Mr. Peabody."

"Uh, yes, of course," Peabody was definitely edgy. "Stick around, Archer. I want to talk to you about this." Then to Miss Bellows: "Show the boy in."

I retired to a chair behind the filing cabinet as Miss Bellows showed Nanu into the room. He sat down beside the registrar's desk. Peabody scanned his application form, toying nervously with a pencil.

"Ah, an exchange student from Zambia University. I see you're interested in athletics."

"Yes, sir," said Nanu.

"What sport are you going out for?"

"All of them," said Nanu.

Peabody broke the pencil.

"All of them, eh?"

Peabody got up and adjusted the kid's chair.

"Are you comfortable there? Would you rather sit over here?" He pointed to his own chair.

Nanu said he was comfortable. Peabody resumed his seat. He had broken into a gentle sweat. He rifled through some papers on his desk, came up with the one he wanted.

"I'm going to ask you a few questions to see if you're qualified for admission," he said.

"Your name?"

"Nanu."

"Correct," said Peabody. "Now the *second* question. This is a historical one. In what year was the Treaty of 1619 signed?"

Nanu looked puzzled.

"1620?" he said.

"That's close enough," beamed Peabody. "It was *ratified* in 1620."

He mopped his brow and continued.

"Now for a mathematical question. Uh, can you do square roots?"

"No," said Nanu.

"Neither can I," laughed Peabody.

He stamped ACCEPTED on the kid's application blank and tossed it into his out-basket. He stood up and shook Nanu's hand.

"Welcome to Merrivale. It's such a pleasure to find a young man who's equally endowed in mind and body."

Nanu walked out the door and left a shaking registrar.

"You handled that very well," I said.

"You really think so?" said Peabody.

"Only one thing — the Treaty of 1619 was ratified in 1622."

Peabody grabbed my arm.

"Does anyone besides you know that?"

The next problem was the matter of a tutor. And that wasn't going to be easy.

The normal tutor is expected to help brush up the slipping student in one, maybe two subjects. But with Nanu's lack of formal education, what we needed was someone who would be willing to devote a lot of time to the kid.

Naturally I thought of Jane Douglas, the one cheerleader who gave some evidence of having cracked a book and whose life didn't seem to revolve around pompons.

I had her meet me in the school cafeteria. But when Milo and I had spelled out our problem, the corners of her pretty mouth turned down.

"I'm sorry, Coach Archer," said Jane. "I couldn't possibly tutor a boy in five subjects. I just don't have the time."

"I thought you wanted to help the team," I said. "Isn't that why you became a cheerleader?"

Jane frowned. "Not really. You see, I'm a sociology major. I just wanted to study crowd psychology. I'm sorry I can't help with your boy."

And she started to get up.

Well, if the girl wouldn't help of her own free will, I'd have to use other methods.

I cut into my steak as though the tutoring problem didn't amount to much.

"Well," I said, "if he survived enslavement, I guess he'll survive this."

"Enslavement?" said the girl, sitting down.

"Let me tell you a little story," I said, flicking a bit of lint from her shoulder. "Picture a young boy growing up in the jungle — held prisoner by the dreaded Arrubi tribe for five years — forced to work their coal mines — "

"Where did this happen?" asked Jane.

"Two hundred feet below the ground."

"How horrible! I had no idea," said Jane.

"Neither did I," said Milo.

I gave him a look.

"Poor kid suffered beyond human endurance," I added.

"Digging for coal in Zambia?" said Jane.

"Me Nanu, you Jane."

"Yes. There is no coal in Zambia."

Jane was reconsidering.

"Well, I suppose I *could* find the time."

"Good, we'll start tomorrow. You'll have to catch him between training sessions."

Just then I saw Nanu coming into the cafeteria.

"Here's your pupil," I said.

The kid crossed to the table and I took care of the introductions.

"Nanu, meet your new tutor, Miss Jane Douglas.

The kid just stared. I've seen love at first sight often enough in movies to know it.

"Me Nanu, you Jane," said the boy.

Milo helped the smitten kid into a seat.

"I guess you two would like to get acquainted — "

"I heard what the Arrubis did to you," said Jane.

"Well," I said, helping him up, "we've got a lot to do."

Heading toward the training field, we ran into some bad medicine.

"Look who's coming," said Milo.

Dean Lacey and his fifth-carbon son Leopold were striding across the campus, looking determined.

"Milo, take the kid over to the locker room. I'll be right along."

"What about the dean?" said Milo.

"Don't worry about the dean. He doesn't have a mind of his own. He'll go any way the wind blows."

Milo and the kid took off, and a second later Dean Lacey and son marched up.

"Well, Archer, I see you're visiting your old home," said the dean.

"No," I said, adjusting the knot on his tie. "As a matter of fact, I've decided to work out my contract."

"That's your privilege," said the dean.

"But you tore up your contract!" said Leopold.

"You'll have to go!" snapped the dean.

"That was a scorecard I tore up. I did it for dramatic effect."

"Well," smiled the dean, "you can't fire a man over a scorecard."

"But he said he was quitting!" whined Leopold.

"You're through!" snapped the dean.

"But I want a winning team as much as you do," I said reasonably.

"His motives are good," said the dean.

"But he can't give us a winning team," said Leopold.

"You're a loser!" growled the dean.

"I'll make a deal with you," I said. "First game I lose, I leave."

"That's fair enough," said the dean.

"I don't buy that!" said Leopold.

"We don't make any deals," said the dean.

"What do you have to lose?" I said. "If I win, you'll have a great season. If I lose, I'll be out."

"We win either way," said the dean to his son. I guess Leopold was stymied by this logic, because before he could answer, his father and I had shaken on the bargain.

"You've got a deal," said the dean.

Leopold fumed.

"I think this is going to work out all right," said the dean pleasantly.

"It looks like trouble to me," said Leopold.

"It's going to be a disaster," said the dean.

Milo didn't think it was too hot a deal either.

"You mean the first game we lose, we have to leave?" said Mister Anguish.

"That's the deal."

Just then the kid came out of the dugout and walked onto the baseball diamond. He looked great in his Merrivale blues, the peaked cap over his unruly shoulder-length hair, a baseball bat riding his brawny shoulder.

I walked over to him and put a paternal arm around him.

"Kid, I'm not going to give you a big pep talk. You're too intelligent for that. I'll just say that we're all counting on you. Now get in there and hit a few."

I motioned Milo to turn on the pitching machine we had out at the mound, as Nanu stepped into the batting cage.

The machine started spitting base-balls at home plate. Nanu brought the bat back and swung. His swing had about as much energy as a burned out battery.

The baseballs buzzed in, and Nanu hit three listless grounders.

"We brought him five thousand miles for this?" said Milo.

I watched another couple of anemic grounders.

"I wonder what's wrong with him," said Milo.

"I know what's wrong with him," I said. "He told me himself in the jungle, but I wouldn't listen. He has no *desire*. He'd rather be throwing coconuts."

"But the kid's a natural," said Milo.

"That's not enough. He has to *want* to be a great athlete. And that's something I can't give him."

Milo moaned.

"The old Archer luck," I said. "If I found Wilt Chamberlain in the jungle, he'd want to be a nuclear physicist!"

I was afraid of what I might say to the kid, so I started off the field.

"Where you going, Coach?" said Milo.

"I've got to think," I said.

Just then Jane Douglas appeared in the empty grandstand, some books under her arm, ready for the kid's first lesson.

That's when it happened.

The kid looks up into the stands, sees the girl, and the next thing you know he is banging those baseballs right off the campus.

"Coach — he's got it!" shouted Milo and turned the knob on the pitching machine.

"I'll speed it up a little," he said.

"Milo — don't touch that machine — it's very sensitive — "

Too late. Baseballs started spewing out of the pitching machine at high speed. They were flying at all corners of the plate, inside and out, high and low, tight and wide.

And Nanu was lashing out, like a man fighting a cobra in a phone booth. He was sending those balls out of the ballpark as fast as they came at him.

"You know, Coach," said Milo, frowning thoughtfully, "I'm just guessing, but I think he plays better when that girl's around."

CHAPTER EIGHT

"In the next few weeks we've got to teach this kid everything there is to know about college sports," I told Milo. And I meant it.

First baseball.

Milo pitching, me coaching at first, Nanu taking his lead off the base. I gave the boy the signal to steal. And off he scampered. Good break, fast getaway.

He takes two steps and then he goes into a diving slide that carries him the rest of the 90 feet to second base.

"I think he started his slide too early," said Milo.

Pole vaulting.

"What's the record for the pole vault?" I asked Milo.

He flipped through the record book.

"Indoor record is 17 feet six inches,

outdoor record is 17 feet 10 inches."

I signalled the kid to give it a try.

He grabbed the pole, raced toward the crossbar, gathering speed along the runway, then vaulted toward the gymnasium ceiling.

He crashed through the skylight.

"He just broke both the indoor and the outdoor record," said Milo.

High hurdles.

Nanu leaping around the track like a gazelle, Milo and I standing beside the track staring at our stopwatches in disbelief.

He's been going at it for forty-eight hours without a letup and is starting to look winded. He comes over to his beloved coach.

"Can I take a break?" he asks.

"You just did," I say.

So that night we try him in a practice game.

Our varsity baseball team, which hasn't won a game in four seasons, is playing the freshmen. I put Nanu in as a pinchhitter in the ninth with the bases loaded.

In comes the pitch. Nanu hits it hard and deep. It's over the center fielder's head. And, believe it or not, the kid just stands and watches the ball fly.

"Run!" I shout.

So Nanu drops his bat, races across the field and tackles the pitcher.

"I think we're pushing him too fast," says Milo.

Up in the grandstand, Jane Douglas and Nanu's tiger are fast asleep.

But the kid is coming along…

Track.

We're watching Nanu throw the discus. He's already handled the javelin and hammer like they were so much breadfruit.

I've been pushing the boy pretty hard.

"Coach," says Milo, "we've been going all day. Can't we get something to eat?"

"You're right," I tell him. "Get me a sandwich."

"How about Nanu?" says Milo.

"No, he doesn't have time to get me a sandwich."

Jane and Harri watch Nanu and Coach Archer discuss Nanu's performance on the field.

Football.

We've gone over some basic plays and the kid has picked them up fast. Great natural instincts.

Now we try the place-kick.

Milo holds the ball at the 10-yard line. I approach the ball slow and easy as Nanu watches me.

"This is what we call a field goal," I explain.

64

And then I kick it through the uprights.

"Now you try it. Put it right through the goalposts."

But Nanu approaches the ball from the wrong side. And the silly kid kicks it through the wrong goalposts.

Ninety yards away.

Enter the villain.

It's a little later and I'm showing Nanu the fine art of the screen pass. Take the snap from center, take three steps back, hold the ball behind your right ear and let it go.

"Now you try it," I say.

Nanu takes the ball from center and sizzles a strike to the tight end. He takes another, sends it to another receiver. And another...

That's when Leopold arrives on the field.

"This kid's sensational," says Milo to Little Mister Trouble.

"He's not bad," sneers Leopold.

And then he turns to Jane, who is standing on the sidelines, waiting for a break so she and Nanu can hit the textbooks.

"Why the sudden interest in foot-ball?" Leopold asks her.

"I have to be here," says Jane. "I tutor Nanu between practice periods."

"Why don't we go out tonight?" asks Leopold, turning on what he must consider to be charm.

"Oh, I can't," says Jane. "I've got a lesson with Nanu."

"Who's teaching what to whom?" sneers Leopold and walks off in a huff, his favorite means of transportation.

"If ever I have a son," says Milo, "I'd like him to beat up Leopold."

As the players trotted into the locker room at the conclusion of practice, Milo was beaming.

"Boy, now we're ready for Broxton! That kid has given the whole team a lift. He's great!"

"He's great all right," I groused. "He's great because she's watching."

"So what?" said Milo. "What's the difference *why* he's great?"

"The difference is everything," I explained. "I want him to play because he wants to win — not just to impress some girl."

Just then a couple of my beauties approached — fullback Gronsky and tackle Carpenter.

"A couple of the fellas want to see you about changing their numbers," mumbled Milo.

"Good sign," I said. "It's the first time they showed a little pride in the uniform."

"But we don't have any budget for alterations."

I said I'd take care of that and motioned Gronsky over.

"Talk to you a minute, Coach?" he said.

I asked him what was up.

"I don't want Number 46 anymore, Coach. I want Number 33."

I grabbed Milo's clipboard.

"Okay, if that's what you want, Gronsky. Only personally, I'm a little disappointed."

"Why, Coach?"

"Well, 46 was my old number. But I'll change it for you — "

"Oh, no, Coach! I'll keep it!"

And off he trotted.

"Talk to you a minute, Coach?" said Carpenter.

"What is it?"

"I've been thinking, Coach. I don't want 59 anymore. I'd like Number 50."

"Wait a minute!" I snapped. "*You're* not supposed to have 59. That's *my* old number. I promised that to Kowalsky."

Carpenter looked stung.

"Why should Kowalsky have it? I've got seniority over Kowalsky. *I* want 59. Let Kowalsky get his own number."

And Carpenter stalked off.

"Wait a minute, Coach," said Milo. "Your old number was 22."

"Quiet," I laughed. "Do you want to get me in trouble?"

Just then, Nanu trotted into the locker room, untying his scrimmage vest.

"We've got a big game with Broxton tomorrow," I told him. "How do you feel?"

"Good," said the kid.

"Don't you have a lesson?"

"Yes, Coach."

"Well, hurry up and change."

Nanu pulled off his scrimmage vest and trotted off, as Milo stared at the number on the boy's back.

It was 22.

CHAPTER NINE

The kid was really coming along. And though I would have been happier if his motivation was something more basic than a pretty girl, I couldn't kick.

The annual game with Broxton was the following day. When I thought of all the humiliations I'd suffered at their hands, it made me bristle. I guess it also made me a little tense. Otherwise I wouldn't have been so hard on Nanu when he walked into the boarding-house an hour past curfew on the evening before the big game.

"Where've you been?" I demanded.

"Jane take Nanu to movies," said the kid.

"Do you know what time it is? It's eleven o'clock. Hannibal conquered Spain, Portugal, and Persia and he was in bed by nine-thirty. Now, get to sleep."

It must have been about midnight that I looked into his room and got a small shock. There was Milo creeping about, opening his window for ventilation, tucking in his blanket, and generally acting like a mother hen to the sleeping kid from the jungle.

I touched my assistant's elbow.

"Milo — I've told you a thousand times. No personal involvement with the athletes. The boy doesn't need a mother. He needs a *coach*. Now get out of here."

Milo preceded me out of the room and scurried off to his own bedroom.

I waited a few seconds, then entered the boy's bedroom.

I finished tucking him in...

Just as I was retreating out the door, his voice froze me in my tracks.

"Good night, Coach," said the kid.

"Oh, good night, champ," I said, like a kid who's been caught at the cookie jar. "If you can't sleep, you know where I'll be."

It must have been nearly three A.M. when I felt a body stretch out next to me on the bed.

Mrs. Petersen watches TV with Harri.

So the kid had a case of nerves after all.

"Couldn't sleep, huh, kid?"

If I had opened my eyes, I would have seen the tiger lying in bed beside me.

I reached out and patted a brawny shoulder.

"Don't worry, they can't hurt us," I said.

My hand brushed a face and I felt some whiskers.

"You know, pretty soon you'll be ready to shave."

The body rolled over.

"Don't take up the whole bed," I said.

I heard a yawn.

"Tired, huh, kid?"

Then a growl.

"I hope you're not coming down with a cold," I said.

The body lashed about with its feet.

"I worked awfully hard getting you ready for this game," I said.

I felt a wet tongue licking my face.

"No, the way to thank me is out on the field."

I felt a head resting on my chest.

"Now look, kid, there's nothing to be nervous about. Remember, you're bigger than they are and you're *stronger* than they are."

That was the point at which Milo came creeping into the darkened room.

"Coach — "

"Yeah, what is it, Milo?"

"The tiger isn't in the kid's room."

"Don't worry about it," I said. "Get some sleep."

Milo shrugged and went off. And, turning to the long body stretched out beside me in the darkness, I said:

"Nanu, you're going to have to do something about that tiger."

The Merrivale commissary was decorated with a bevy of "Beat Broxton" signs and there was quite a festive air about this pregame breakfast.

I'd seen those "Beat Broxton" signs before, but this was the first time I thought we might actually do it.

So did the team. They were seated at two long tables in an alcove of the commissary. I sat at the head of one of them, flanked by Milo and Nanu.

"Now remember what I told you, kid. Stay behind your blockers."

I was giving him a little pregame refresher course and working off a little of my own excess excitement. One of my gestures was a little too excessive. I knocked over a saltshaker.

"Oh boy," said Milo, and threw a pinch of salt over his shoulder.

"Why you do that?" asked Nanu.

"When you spill salt, it's a bad omen," said Milo.

That's all I needed. Milo giving our boy a case of superstitious nerves right before the big game.

"Milo, don't upset the kid."

"Is it bad luck?" Nanu asked me.

I had to improvise.

"Not if the salt falls on a checkered tablecloth," I said. The kid smiled with relief.

"Look, Coach," said Milo, pointing. "A broken mirror. Now *that* certainly means bad luck."

"Unless you break a glass," I said and smashed my water glass on the table.

Milo nodded and smashed his own water glass.

Nanu followed suit with his.

By now the table was a lake of broken crystal. But at least the kid looked contented.

"The glass cancels the mirror and the tablecloth cancels the salt," I said.

Milo pointed to a lowered window shade.

"Shade down — prepare to frown."

I snapped the shade aloft.

"Shade up — winner's cup."

"Do you realize there are thirteen people eating at this table?" said Milo.

"The waiter makes fourteen," I said.

"But he's not eating!"

"Milo right," said the kid. I guess his upbringing had made him susceptible to superstitious nonsense.

"Now look, kid," I said, "superstition isn't going to win or lose this game. What you *do* out there is what's going to decide the game."

I turned to Milo.

"Now, I don't want to hear any more about your silly superstitions."

Harri chaperones Nanu during an outing with Jane.

Nanu and Jane have left him, so Harri creates his own diversion. The cops don't seem amused.

Just then a reporter from the school paper bent over me, pencil poised over pad.

"Hey, Coach — do you have a prediction about today's game?"

"I think we can take 'em," I said and knocked wood.

As Milo and I entered the coaches' room that adjoins the big locker room, I had a sense of elation — a feeling that we were finally going to lick the team that shoved our face in the mud year after year.

"Let's use a 6-2-2-1 defense for the first quarter and see if they penetrate," I said, rubbing my forehead.

"You okay, Coach?"

"Just a little headache. Pregame nerves."

Milo produced a bottle from the first-aid cabinet.

"Take a couple of aspirin."

I looked at the bottle with its distinctive label and grabbed it.

"You want the kid to see this? He'll hop a plane for home!"

I tossed the bottle in a wastebasket and crossed into the locker room. As I did, I noticed the dean's son, Leopold Lacey, skulking in the corridor. I had the uncomfortable feeling that he had been listening to our conversation...

The team was waiting for me in the locker room.

"Fellas," I said, "I'm not going to give you a big pep talk. You're too intelligent for that. I'm not going to try to stir your emotions. I'm not going to kid you. You know this is just another football game."

Then I whirled and jabbed my finger at them.

"But let me tell you this — I want you to go out there and drive drive drive! I want you to go go go! And I want you to win!"

The varsity leaped up and crowded out the door, leaving Milo and me alone in the silent locker room.

"Well, what do you think?" I said.

"I still think you should've given them a pep talk," said Milo.

As we waited for the opening kickoff, I checked to see that Jane Douglas was in her accustomed position among the cheerleaders, so Nanu could see her from the field. She was our guarantee of a top-performing quarterback. She was there.

I noticed something else that was less reassuring. Our water boy, Freddie, was nowhere to be seen. In his place, wearing Freddie's team sweater, was the Lacey kid.

"Where's Freddie?" I asked him.

"He's under the weather, Coach," said Leopold. "He asked me to stand in for him."

I nodded doubtfully and returned to the bench.

I had converted Nanu's tiger into the team mascot and he stood on the sidelines straining at a leash held by a nervous cheerleader.

Across the field, the Broxton ram was staring arrogantly across at us.

The teams took the field, the grandstands quieted for the "National Anthem," and then the referee's whistle blew the game into action. Broxton kicked off and Nanu received the ball.

He took two steps and fell flat on his face.

Nanu dropped the ball and a Broxton player recovered and ran for a touchdown. Six seconds and six nothing, Broxton.

Milo was wearing his ulcerous look.

"Just a touch of the jitters," I said. "He'll be all right."

The defensive team went in and Nanu came off. Leopold acted very solicitous to the kid, even handed him a towel to wipe off his hands.

Broxton scored again against our weak defensive line, and Broxton led 14 to nothing.

Nanu went back in to receive the next Broxton kickoff and *again* fell on his face. This time he held onto the ball.

Coming out of the huddle on first down, Nanu called a pass play. He faded back and tried to throw. But he couldn't seem to get rid of the ball. It clung to his fingers, almost as though the ball were glued to his hand.

By now the fans were turning nasty. A chorus of boos was rising.

The tiger turned and growled at the grandstand.

The fans quieted down fast.

I looked over at Leopold and decided he was the rotten kid I always thought him to be. Here we were 14 points down, and he was sitting on the sidelines, sprinkling pepper on a sandwich!

The ball went over to Broxton on a fumble and Nanu returned to the bench.

"Don't let 'em throw you, champ," I said. "Hang in there."

The ball came back to Merrivale and the offensive team returned to the field. Leopold handed Nanu his helmet which the kid clamped back onto his head.

As Nanu ran onto the field, he sneezed. Going into the huddle he sneezed again, and as he called the signals he sneezed again.

He faded back for a pass. As he was about to release the ball, he sneezed again. The pass fell short and was intercepted for another Broxton touchdown.

The third of the day.

It seemed like hours later, but it was just deep in the fourth quarter. Merrivale was losing by 48 points and I was thinking about a career in mutual funds.

Leopold had reverted to form. He stood beside me, smirking unpleasantly.

"I wonder what Jane thinks of her boy from the jungle now," he said.

Then I noticed that Nanu was removing his helmet and tossing it off the field.

"I guess he finds it too confining," I said.

But Leopold looked shaken.

"What's he doing?" said Leopold in a panic.

And then I remembered. Leopold holding that pepper shaker — Leopold handing Nanu his helmet — Nanu sneezing his head off and losing control of the ball.

Then I noticed the shoes. Nanu was pulling them off and tossing them onto the sidelines.

"He's getting rid of his shoes!" moaned Leopold.

And then I remembered something else. Leopold skulking around the locker room before the game — and Nanu sliding over the field as though there were no cleats on his shoes — as though someone had applied a layer of grease to his soles.

And I remembered Leopold handing a towel to Nanu — and a moment later, the football sticking like glue to the boy's hand.

It all added up at once. And the look I gave Leopold must have conveyed my thinking. He edged out of reach.

Suddenly the roar of the crowd brought my attention back to the field. A barefoot, helmetless Nanu, his hair flying in the wind, was racing through the Broxton team, heading for the goal line.

Touchdown.

The kid caught fire.

With eight minutes to play, Nanu started hitting with passes, running like lightning, knocking the Broxton linemen rump over teakettle, rolling up one touchdown after another. With three minutes to play, the scoreboard read Broxton 48, Merrivale 45.

I kept one eye on Leopold. He wasn't going to do anything more to sabotage my boy! He was now far from the Merrivale bench. I could see him handing a note to an usher and pointing to the cheerleaders.

I turned my attention back to the playing field. There was plenty of time for the final touchdown that would put Merrivale ahead and put the game on ice.

Merrivale had the ball after Nanu intercepted a Broxton pass.

The kid came out of the huddle and looked over toward the sidelines. And then it happened.

His face fell as though he had been hit between the eyes with a rock. And, as he stood there, the Broxton line flooded in and decked him brutally.

I knew what that look meant. I looked over at the cheerleading section.

"She isn't there," I said.

"But why would she leave?" said Milo.

Then I remembered the note to the usher and the dean's son pointing to the cheerleaders.

"Leopold must have figured out that the kid needs her for inspiration. The way he looks over there before every play, it wouldn't take a genius to figure it out. Leopold must've lured her out of the way."

"I'll find her!" said Milo.

"In a crowd like this? Forget it. There's no time."

Now the Broxton line was taking out their resentment against the boy who had made them look so bad. With all

Harri finds a comfortable spot for an afternoon snooze.

the zest gone from Nanu, they were piling on him unmercifully.

On an end run, they knocked him
clear into his own bench. As the referee
pulled them off, one of the Broxton
players "accidentally" elbowed the kid
in the jaw.

"Go back to the jungle, nature boy," said the Broxton kid.

Milo looked as anguished as I felt.

"It's no good," I told Milo. "I knew we shouldn't have depended on the girl. He needs a desire to *win*. That's what makes a champion. And that's something he's got to find for himself."

Out on the field, the Broxton line was piling on Nanu again.

"Well, if I can't give him the will to win," I said, "the least I can do is keep him from getting killed. I'm taking him out."

Milo grabbed me. "But, Coach, he might snap out of it. He's our only chance — "

"Gronsky — in for Nanu."

Gronsky trotted onto the field.

"Nanu — out," Gronsky yelled.

The kid returned to the bench looking confused and angry, and sat down next to Milo.

"You all right?" asked Milo. "The coach was worried about you."

"Coach not worried about me," said Nanu. "Coach just worried about *winning*."

Milo's temper flared.

"Forget it, Milo."

"No, I won't forget it." He turned on the kid. "Not worried about you! The coach just threw away his job to keep you from getting hurt."

"Nanu not understand."

"If we lose this game, the coach loses his job. But he's willing to lose it to protect you. That's how much he cares about you."

Nanu considered this a moment, then stood up and rushed out onto the field.

"Gronsky — out," shouted Nanu.

The clock showed fifteen seconds remaining in the game, with Merrivale trailing by three points.

The kid called a signal for a long pass.

I knew it wouldn't do any good. Broxton had each of our receivers covered like blankets. Nanu could throw all the long passes he wanted, but there was no one on the Merrivale squad to catch them.

With two seconds on the clock, the kid took the snap from center and passed deep down the field.

Then he did it. I still don't believe it, but he did it. He ran around his own end, raced down the sidelines, passing both teams. Then he cut back to the center of the field and caught his own pass.

That's when the tiger broke loose.

The last twenty yards of Nanu's run were along the sidelines, with his tiger right beside him.

Nanu crossed the goal line, the scoreboard registered 51 for Merrivale to Broxton's 48, and the gun sounded ending the game.

The stands went wild.

Merrivale had actually beaten Broxton.

Milo was in a frenzy.

"Jane got back just in time!" he said.

We looked over at the sidelines.

"But she's not there — " said Milo, showing surprise.

"He's done it!" I said. "We've got ourselves a champion."

Dean Lacey was all over me, glowing with pride, pounding my back.

"Congratulations, Archer. I knew you could do it. I always had the utmost confidence in you."

"You might talk to your son," snapped Milo. "He was doing all he could to sabotage the team."

Milo handed the dean one of Nanu's shoes. Its cleats had been cut off. The dean motioned his son to the bench, fixed him with an icy stare.

"Leopold, it has been called to my attention that someone has been sabotaging our team. Now, I know you've cheated on exams, stolen money from the faculty fund, and forged my name on checks. Tell me, Leopold — are you also responsible for this?"

"No, Father," said Leopold.

"That's good enough for me, son," said the dean.

Milo and I crossed the field which by now was swarming with happy Merrivale students and alumni.

Nanu's teammates had hoisted the kid up on their shoulders. It was a great moment.

As we crossed toward the boy, the Broxton coach intercepted me.

"Archer — you've got to do something — "

"What's the matter?"

"What's the matter! I'll tell you what's the matter. Your mascot *ate* our mascot."

CHAPTER TEN

The next few months were a series of broken records and screaming headlines.

Nanu Scores 50 Points
Against Medfield Eleven

Nanu Breaks Basket-
ball Scoring Record

Nanu Bats .480 for
Merrivale Nine

And then the sign that Nanu and Merrivale had really arrived. The kid became the subject of TV sports specials.

They filmed one of the interviews in my office at the college.

Behind the TV camera was sportscaster Jim McKay. Milo was standing beside me.

"This is Jim McKay at Merrivale. Today the eyes of the sporting world are focused on this tiny college in America's heartland. The reason? a boy named Nanu who came out of the jungles of Africa to become the most versatile athlete in American college history. The two men most responsible for Nanu's fantastic success are his head coach and mentor, Sam Archer, and Archer's loyal assistant, Milo Jackson...

"Coach — tell us about that moment when you first discovered Nanu. How did you feel?"

"Fantastic," said Milo. "I knew right away we had something special."

"Was it difficult teaching him the various sports?" asked McKay.

"Well — " I began.

"You do what you can," said Milo. "After all, he comes from a primitive society."

I stared at Milo.

"What's the boy like off the field?"

"Nicest kid you ever want to meet, Jim. I'm like a father to him."

"What does the future hold for the boy?" asked McKay.

Milo sat down on the edge of my desk.

"We can write our own ticket."

"Coach Archer," said McKay, "what are *your* plans for the future?"

I considered. "First thing I'm going to do is get myself a new assistant."

And Milo jumped off the desk.

"And now," continued McKay, "our African correspondent, Kurt Newman, talks on TV to the boy's godfather, a tribal witch doctor named Gazenga, in Zambia."

We watched on the monitor as the technicians screened a film for us that had been taken a week before. There on the screen was the correspondent talking to Gazenga in his mountain cave.

"What do you think of your godson's success?" asked the correspondent.

"Boy belongs in jungle," snapped Gazenga. I guess he didn't think too much of the kid's success. Or maybe he just missed him.

"Boy should never have left jungle," added the witch doctor.

Was he always interested in athletics?" asked the correspondent.

"Gazenga cannot talk now. Must administer jungle justice. One of these men is guilty of crime. Both will drink poison. Guilty man will die."

The correspondent watched expectantly as first one man drank, then the other. After a long beat the correspondent pitched forward on his face.

CHAPTER ELEVEN

I found them in the Merrivale Record Shop. Nanu was in one of the booths, listening to music on a pair of earphones. Milo was flipping through a pile of old Glenn Miller records.

"I've been looking all over for you," I said. "What's the kid doing?"

"Listening to some records of African music."

"I've got great news for him. I'm entering him in the most important track meet in the country. He may be a little nervous, so back me up in whatever I say. We've got to build his confidence."

"Gotcha, Coach."

We entered the listening booth. I sat down opposite the kid and turned down the volume. Milo stood by the door.

"Nanu, I've got great news. I'm entering you in the NCAA Championships."

"He's not ready," said Milo.

I turned and stared.

"What did you say?"

"He's not ready."

I turned back to the kid.

"There are eighteen events and I'm entering you in *every one of them!*"

"He'll never do it," said Milo.

"Eighteen?" said Nanu. Milo's uncertainty was contagious.

"Now listen kid," I said. "I'll tell you something else. I'm betting you'll *win every event.*"

"He'll be lucky to finish," said Milo.

I stared at my assistant, then turned back to the kid.

"Not only that. You're going to break the *record* in every event."

"Couldn't do it in a million years," said Milo.

"Can Nanu do all that?" asked the kid.

"Of course you can. We leave tomorrow."

I handed Nanu the record albums that were lying by the turntable.

"Take these over to the cashier."

The moment the kid was gone, I turned on Milo.

"I told you to back me up to build the kid's confidence! Instead you undercut everything I said. Why did you *do* that?"

"I didn't want to give him a big head," said Milo.

There was a fresh wind whipping Merrivale Airport the next morning. It nearly blew the newspaper out of my hand.

The headline read: Nanu Leaves for NGAA. And the subhead read: Star Athlete to Compete in All Events.

As Milo, the kid, and I approached our plane, a group of reporters dogged us right up to the foot of the ramp.

"Hey, Sam, is Nanu ready for the NCAA meet?"

"He's ready," I said.

"Is it true he's going for a record in every event?"

"That's right."

"What kind of condition is he in?"

"Sorry, fellas," I said, "we've got to get aboard."

Nanu and I started up the ramp.

"The boy's in tip-top shape..."

It was Milo at the foot of the ramp,

chatting with the reporters.

"With any luck at all, we should — "

I grabbed him and yanked him up the steps.

"Well, champ," I said to the kid, "we're on our way. Nothing can stop us now." We stepped into the airliner.

Then, just before the cabin door slammed shut, I noticed a man emerging from the plane that had just landed opposite ours.

It was Gazenga.

I took Milo aside and told him what I had seen.

"Oh yeah," said Milo complacently. "I read something about that in the school paper."

"You what!"

I rifled through the paper. There it was, buried on a back page: Merrivale Medical School to Welcome Dr. Gazenga.

The subheadline read: African Witch Doctor to Lecture on Tribal Medicine.

"It's probably just a coincidence," said Milo.

"I'd like to believe that," I said. "And maybe I could, if it weren't for the guy

who was at the foot of the ramp when
Gazenga stepped out."

"Who was that?"

"Leopold Lacey," I said.

Gazenga arrives from Africa. Leopold has sent for him.

CHAPTER TWELVE

By the time we had the kid safely deposited in his room at the Ambassador Hotel, I had about convinced myself that we could get him through the NCAA track meet without interference from Leopold or any imported witch doctors.

But I still wasn't taking any chances.

I had Milo check Nanu's room every ten minutes while I did some planning for the track meet that began the following day.

"What's the kid doing now?" I asked Milo for the umpteenth time as we sat in the hotel bar.

"Taking a nap."

"I'd better see that he's all right."

As I went away Milo continued to check the list of events in which Nanu was entered. Later he told me a really weird story. He was sitting there mumbling to himself....

"High jump ... long jump ... pole vault ... 440 meter ... 100-yard dash ... high hurdles ... javelin throw ... hammer throw ... discus throw ...."

Suddenly he looked up from his notes and there was the witch doctor.

"Gazenga!"

Something landed on the table in front of him.

It was an empty aspirin bottle.

"Here is your life-saving medicine," sneered Gazenga. "A headache remedy! I've come to take the boy home."

"Now wait a minute — "

"Fortunately, there is one man in your college who is devoted to the boy's welfare. Leopold Lacey."

"Leopold — "

"He told me of the deception you practiced on the boy to bring him to America. And he told me how you and Archer are exploiting him — pushing him beyond the limits of human endurance — to feed your own despicable drive to success."

"Now, there's no reason we can't dis-

Leopold tells Gazenga that his godson Nanu is in peril and that the two Merrivale coaches are responsible.

cuss this like civilized human beings," Milo said, adjusting Gazenga's necklaces. "Sit down — let's have a drink."

He gestured to a waiter as Gazenga sat.

"I'll have an old-fashioned. What are you drinking, Gazenga?"

"Scorpion's blood with the eye of a leopard," said the witch doctor.

"Make that two old-fashioneds."

The waiter went away shaking his head.

"You stole the boy from his people," continued Gazenga.

The waiter deposited the drinks and hurried off.

"Just a minute, Gazenga," Milo said. "This is the land of opportunity. Nanu found it in sports. You could find it in *your* profession." (He wondered what was keeping me.)

"Nonsense."

"It's true. Americans *love* doctors. There's real opportunity for you here."

"You mean in medicine?"

"No, in television."

Milo was pulling out all the stops. He pointed to a distinguished looking guy in a dinner jacket, standing by the entrance.

"You see that man? He's an important television executive."

He waved and the guy waved back.

"He's a good friend of mine," Milo continued. "He could make you a TV star."

"But Gazenga know nothing about such things."

"It's simple. You go to a studio and you talk in front of a camera."

"What is camera?"

"A camera is the thing that carries your picture all over the country. You just talk into a microphone."

"What is microphone?"

"A microphone is the thing that carries the sound of your voice to the TV sets."

"What is TV set?"

"A TV set is a box where your picture appears," Milo explained.

"Will this be film or tape?" asked Gazenga.

"Both," said Milo. "And that man over there could make it happen."

And so, just then, the guy in the dinner jacket comes through the door carrying a tray of drinks.

"A waiter!" shouted Gazenga. "More lies! I'm taking the boy!"

He got up to leave.

"Don't you go near him — "

"I warn you. Do not stand in my way. The power of my voodoo is great."

Milo had about had it with his jungle silliness.

"Now listen. You may impress your tribe with that mumbo jumbo, but you don't impress me."

Gazenga stared at Milo, made some odd gestures, mouthed some odd syllables.

"You're not in Africa now," Milo reminded him.

Milo is about to be mesmerized by Gazenga's voodoo.

And then he noticed it. The little cocktail table looked like a vast desert — and Gazenga looked like a monstrous giant! The way he judged it, by a quick comparison with his old-fashioned glass, he was now about three inches tall.

"I suppose you think this proves something," Milo said.

"Now I shall get Nanu," said Gazenga evenly.

"Don't touch that boy!" Milo shouted. He shook his tiny fist up at him.

Gazenga has made Milo three inches tall and dropped him into a cocktail glass.

"You go near him and you'll answer to me!"

Gazenga didn't seem too disturbed by the threat. He plucked Milo off his chair and held him over the old-fashioned glass.

"Cool off, Milo," he said, and dropped him into the glass.

Gazenga marched out of the room like a man with a mission.

Meanwhile Milo was struggling to keep from drowning. The trouble was he couldn't get a grip on the ice cubes.

Milo can't get a grip on the ice cubes but wonders whether the swizzle stick will be useful.

He grabbed the swizzle stick and tried using it as a mountain climber uses an alpenstock. He managed to climb to the brink of the glass and drop to the table below.

He knew he had to warn Nanu and me, and he didn't have much time to do it in.

He managed to drop from the table top to the chair cushion. But before he could move further, a woman was ushered to the now vacant table and he saw a huge shape lowering itself toward him. The lady was about to sit down.

Leaping just in time, Milo grabbed the edge of the cushion and held on for dear life. Then he managed to slide down the chair leg to the floor below.

"This is the last time I drink with a witch doctor," he said to himself.

He hurried out of the bar as fast as he could, considering his size, and into the teeming hotel lobby.

Between the NCAA athletes staying at the hotel and a couple of conventions, the lobby was crowded with guests registering and arriving. He had the feeling that any minute he might be flattened underfoot.

He threaded his way through a forest of feet and headed for the elevator, which seemed miles away.

Suddenly a suitcase came bearing down on him, carried by a bellhop. Leaping out of the way, just in time to avoid being clobbered, he landed behind a chair.

"Got to get to the kid," he thought to himself.

He started across the lobby again. Then suddenly he heard a loud whirring sound and felt himself being caught up in a powerful air current that was pulling him backward.

He looked up and saw a chambermaid with a vacuum cleaner.

Milo fought the suction as best he could, but was slowly being drawn in toward the mouth of the vacuum cleaner. He had to grab a chair leg to keep from being sucked into the mechanism.

As he held on, the maid pushed the machine past him. And now the exhaust from the machine suddenly blew him high into the air.

He came to rest in the soft brown earth of a potted palm. He got to his feet, somewhat dazed by his journey. From his perspective, the palm looked lush and towering.

"I'm back in the jungle," Milo said to himself.

He looked off to the left and saw a heavy set conventioneer seated next to the plant. He was reading a newspaper and smoking a huge cigar. Then, without looking up, the clown reached over and stubbed out his cigar in the dirt, not two inches from where Milo stood.

The smoke billowed around him. He covered his mouth with his handkerchief, but still nearly passed out from the fumes.

"That settles it, I quit smoking," Milo thought.

But the worst was yet to come.

Suddenly he found himself in the midst of a tropical thunderstorm. As the torrential rain poured down, he looked around for the cause. Another chambermaid was watering the plant!

Enough was enough.

He leaped from the potted palm to a nearby coffee table, then looked down toward the floor. It appeared to be a dangerous drop.

Looking about the table he spotted the conventioneer's hat. It gave him an idea. He pulled the feather out of the hatband and, holding it tightly, leaped to the floor. The feather acted like a parachute to slow his fall.

But he hadn't counted on the middle-aged lady seated on the sofa beside the conventioneer. She opened a large purse, removed her eyeglasses and put the open purse on the floor beside the sofa.

And Milo drifted into the open purse...

Where he found himself surrounded by the assorted paraphernalia of a lady's handbag. Lipstick. Compact. Keys. Wallet. Nail polish. Emery boards. Comb and brush. Spool of thread. Kleenex. Unmailed letter. Cigarettes. Address book...

He fought his way through the assortment, trying to get a foothold on the constantly shifting objects, but couldn't find a firm footing.

When he wasn't being smothered by Kleenex tissue, he was fighting to become unstuck from an airmail stamp.

Deep at the bottom of a ladies' handbag, the three-inch-high Milo contemplates the assorted paraphernalia around him.

When he accidentally opened a vial of cold capsules, thousands of tiny time capsules came cascading over his head.

Then came an idea. Seizing a threaded needle he hurled it like a javelin at the top of the purse. It stuck. He used the thread to pull himself up the inside of the purse.

This brought him to the top of the handbag. Once there, he bound a pair of emery boards to his feet with thread, and used them as skis to slide down the sloping side of the purse to the floor.

So far so good. But this was taking too

Seizing the threaded needle, Milo gets ready to hurl it over the top of the bag.

much time. He was beginning to feel he'd never get to the kid's room.

"I'd better call him," he thought. "Now, where are those housephones?"

He could see a row of phones on a ledge in the lobby alcove. Hurrying across the lobby of the alcove, he climbed a telephone wire to the ledge, and climbed onto the telephone dial.

Room 369. Now to dial....

He pushed the huge receiver off its cradle so that it lay on the counter, then pulled the dial until the "three" reached the stop position.

Then he released it. The dial spun back to neutral, carrying Milo with it and hurling him off the phone.

Again Milo climbed onto the dial, pulling it forward from the "six." When he released the dial this time, it nearly threw him off the ledge.

He went back again to dial the "nine." This time the dial spun nearly 360 degrees. Milo held on for dear life.

"Why couldn't he have been in Room 111?" was Milo's thought.

But the connection was made. He could hear a loud intermittent buzzing from the receiver.

He squatted on the telephone waiting for the connection to be made.

After what seemed an eternity, Milo heard my voice.

"Hello?"

"Hello — this is Milo!" he shouted.

"Where are you, Milo?"

"I'm on the phone," Milo said. "Check the kid."

Milo struggles to get the phone off the hook. He *must* call Archer.

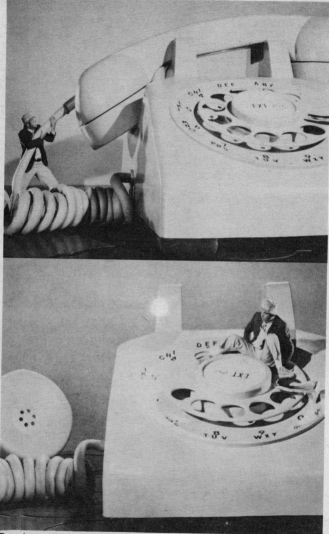

Receiver off the hook, Milo pulls the dial into the right position.

Milo waited while I checked the boy's room.

"He's not there," I said, suddenly very anxious.

"Come down to the lobby - -"

Before Milo could say another word, he was being lifted into the air by the long black fingers of Gazenga.

"What did you do with the kid?" Milo demanded.

"Where are you, Coach?" Milo shouts.

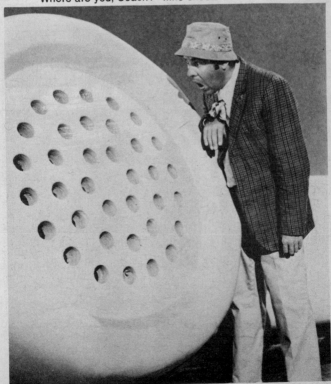

Gazenga's long fingers lift Milo into the air.

Back to his normal size, Milo tells Archer how it feels to be three inches tall.

"When I told him of your treachery, he ran from the hotel," said Gazenga.

"I've got to find him!" Milo said. "He's never been alone in the city before."

This made sense even to a Zambian witch doctor. He snapped his fingers and Milo resumed his normal size.

"Very well," said the witch doctor, "but he will never come back with you."

Milo was at the entrance to the hotel when I came out. So was the doorman.

He told me that my nature boy had headed into the park that faced the hotel. Milo and I dashed across the street and into the park.

"Look, Coach — Nanu's shoe."

Sure enough, it was one of Nanu's loafers, lying on the grass. Twenty feet ahead was the other one.

Further on was his shirt, his tie, his socks and trousers. Nanu was shedding all the signs of civilization — and providing us with a trail.

His undershirt was beside a sign that read: "TO ZOO."

We trotted the rest of the way to the park zoo. And there, across a moat, atop a boulder in the tiger's area, wearing only the loincloth in which I had first seen him, was Nanu.

"I've got to talk to you," I said. "Come down here."

The kid leaped lightly to the ground and stared sullenly at me.

"You lied to Nanu. You told him he saved your life."

"You *did* save my life, kid. The aspirin didn't, but you did."

"Nanu not save your life."

"Yes you did. When I came to the jungle, my life as a coach was over. But you changed all that."

He wasn't buying.

"Why you take Nanu from jungle?" he said bitterly.

"Try to understand, kid. I wanted the world's greatest athlete — and you're close to being that now."

"Is that so important?"

"Important! Today you were going to try to win every event in a track meet! That's never been done before. Only one man ever attempted it. Jim Thorpe — and he failed."

"If that's so important it made you lie, then Nanu want no part of it."

He had me there.

"Well, kid, sometimes people want something so badly they'll do the wrong thing to get it. I hope some day you'll understand that. Good-bye, champ."

I rejoined Milo.

"Is he coming, Coach?"

"No."

"You're gonna let him leave?"

"We'll get along without him. We did all right before he came along."

"Yeah, we always lost."

We walked off, deep in gloom. We passed a group of kids kicking a football around on the grass. As we passed them, I heard the hard, crisp sound of foot connecting with pigskin. I turned around and looked upward.

Flying through the air, in a high, soaring trajectory, was the football. No kid ever kicked a ball that high. Following the flight of the ball was the boy who had kicked it.

Nanu ran up to us.

"What did Jim Thorpe do wrong?" he asked.

I laughed.

"He didn't have me for a coach," I said, and we trotted back toward the hotel.

118

CHAPTER THIRTEEN

Out on the field, the athletes were lined up according to college.

"Today," said the chief judge over the loudspeaker system, "we welcome the cream of the youth of America to the Fiftieth NCAA Track and Field Championships. The country's greatest colleges have sent their finest athletes to compete here today. I'd like to introduce each of these contingents.

"First — Notre Dame."

A group of sixteen young men in blue and gold stepped forward.

"Ohio State."

Another group of athletes stepped forward.

"Alabama."

Another group.

"Yale."

Still another group.

"Merrivale."

Nanu stepped forward.

"This is a big day, kid."

I had taken the boy aside as we waited for the first event.

"I want you to give it your best."

"Why is this meet so important to you, Coach?"

"Why is it important?" I said, adjusting the zipper on his windbreaker. "Let me tell you a little story. Picture a young black boy growing up in the ghetto. Life is a deadend street —

"Then one day he gets his big chance — a chance to stand the world on its ear — break all the records and change all the history books. That's why it's important."

"Athletes assemble!" called the loudspeaker and Nanu trotted off.

Milo joined me.

"Coach, that young black boy from the ghetto — "

"Yes, Milo?"

"That boy was you."

"No, it was Harry Belafonte."

The first event was the javelin throw.

Nanu stood in the center of the javelin circle, holding the long spearlike instrument.

"The record for the javelin throw is 270 feet eight inches," Milo reminded me.

"Nanu of Merrivale — " said the judge.

Nanu wound up and hurled the javelin.

"Eighty-two feet," called the judge.

High in the stands at the NCAA tournament, Gazenga, egged on by Leopold, prepares the magic that will insure Nanu's defeat.

What you call a horrible performance.

Nanu wound up, hurled the javelin in his second try. It flew an even shorter distance.

"Fifty-three feet," called the judge.

Milo stared his puzzlement at me, as Nanu took his third try. This time the javelin came hurtling back at us and we had to jump to avoid being skewered.

The next event was the shot put.

"Nanu of Merrivale — " called the judge.

Nanu wound up to throw the shot put, and suddenly went spinning round like a top. He crashed dizzily into the row of judges.

Milo and I rushed forward to help him up.

"What's the matter, champ?"

"I don't know — "

"Nanu of Merrivale — the discus throw," called the judge.

We hurried him over to the next event.

The kid prepared to hurl the discus. Then as he twirled for the throw, he started screwing himself into the ground!

The voodoo spell is working. Nanu zips backward instead of forward in the broad jump.

He finally released the discus.

"Ten feet," shouted the judge.

"Something very wrong, Coach," said Nanu.

"Yeah, but it's not you, kid. You couldn't be this bad if you tried. It's got to be Gazenga."

Nanu nodded his agreement.

"If we only knew where he was, we might be able to stop him," I said.

"Godfather somewhere near," said Nanu. "He have to *see* Nanu to make such strong magic."

"Are you sure of that?"

"Nanu sure."

"Then we still have a fighting chance. You keep trying. Milo and I will search for Gazenga in the stands."

What I didn't say was that it was a big stadium and I didn't hold out much hope of finding one angry witch doctor.

As Milo and I roamed the stands, I occasionally stopped to look down on the field. Every time I did, I saw Nanu squirming on the tip of Gazenga's magic.

The judge was announcing "Last call for the 880," but I knew the meet was over for Nanu. Milo and I returned to him in the arena.

"It's no good, kid. We can't find him anywhere. Too many people. I'm afraid there's just no way."

"There's *got* to be a way — " said Milo.

"Well, kid, if you have to lose, try to lose with dignity."

Nanu crossed the track and took up his position for the 880-meter race. The starter's gun exploded and the runners broke from the starting line.

All except Nanu. He found himself running full speed in place. The ground under his feet was a treadmill. More voodoo!

"I've got it!" said Milo. "A good luck piece. He's gotta carry a good luck piece. It might work against the voodoo."

I could feel my whole world coming down around my ears. Nanu being destroyed by his witch doctor godfather. And poor panicky Milo scrabbling through his pockets for a good luck piece! Weirdo.

Milo was digging all sorts of superstitious junk out of his pockets.

"Rabbit's foot...lucky skate key... four-leaf clover...lucky coin..."

Then he produced Nanu's voodoo doll. The one I had been examining in Nanu's bedroom.

"Coach — I've got it!" shouted Milo. "I've really got it."

He shoved a couple of feathers into the doll's headband, making it resemble the witch doctor's headdress.

"I've really got it — " shouted Milo.

"Leave me alone, will you? Things are tough enough."

Milo kept waving the darn voodoo doll under my nose in a very irritating way.

"Coach, you don't understand — "

"Milo, will you shut up! I've got to think!"

"Will you just look!"

Again he waved the little monstrosity under my nose. I had had it! I grabbed the doll and tossed it over my shoulder.

Up in the stands there was a commotion. A man had suddenly gone flying out of his seat and into the air.

The doll came down in a water bucket.

There was a shriek from the stands as

Trying to overcome Gazenga's voodoo, Milo concentrates on a good luck piece.

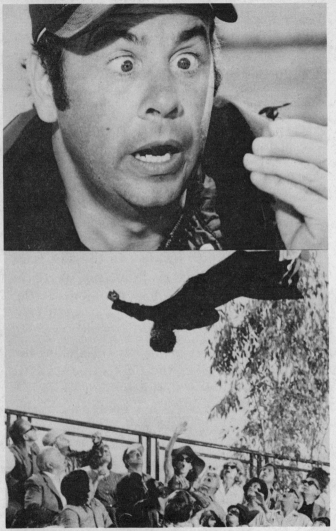

Consternation in the stands! Gazenga suddenly flies out of his seat into the air. Milo's magic is working!

the flying man came down in the Olympic swimming pool next to the stadium.

"A new unofficial high-diving record!" announced the judge.

Suddenly Nanu started running.

"Feels better now," he shouted over his shoulder.

"What happened?" I demanded of Milo.

He held up the water bucket so I could see the doll floating there.

"The voodoo doll. It broke Gazenga's spell!"

Nanu was rapidly making up the ground on the runners in the 880, and the crowd was responding. Within thirty seconds he had taken over the lead and was running away with the race.

Milo looked grim. "It's a shame he did so bad with the field events. He'll never have time to finish them all now."

"Milo, the way he's going, he could take it all. If there was only one more time — "

By the NCAA rules, Nanu was entitled to three tries at each field event. The problem was that time was running out. The events were virtually consecutive.

Nanu starts winning! Freed from Gazenga's black magic,
he breaks all NCAA standing records.

And that's when I got my idea.

I grabbed a field judge's golf cart and took off across the infield toward Nanu, who was still speeding along in the 880. I pulled up alongside him, keeping pace with his long strides.

"Just listen to me, kid. Save your breath for the race."

He nodded.

"There's very little time and we have a lot left to do, understand?"

He nodded again.

"After you win this race, you can't stop running. Look for Milo and run right to him. He'll be set to get you to your next field event. After that, we'll play it by ear. Okay?"

He nodded again and I pulled the golf cart away, leaving him to his running.

I left the golf cart where I found it, just as Nanu broke the tape a good 40 feet ahead of the field.

As he did, I was there playing traffic cop. Nanu kept running full tilt toward Milo.

Across the field the announcer was saying, "Athletes for the 440, please...last event of the meet."

I ignored it. Nanu had lots to do

before the 440 if he was to win in every event.

Milo was holding up a blackboard which read: This Way to High Jump with an arrow. Then he spun the card around and it read: GOOD LUCK!

Nanu approached the high jump at high speed and took off.

I trotted along behind him and tossed a javelin in the air. Landing from the high jump, Nanu caught it on the run, trotted into the circle, and hurled it in the air.

As the fans watched its flight, Milo tossed the kid the shot put. As he caught it, Milo and I each grabbed an elbow and propelled him into the shot-put ring. Nanu promptly went into his throw. The shot put sailed toward the horizon.

Before it landed, Nanu was approaching the pole vault. I tossed him the pole as he raced down the track toward the crossbar. As he ran, Milo was rolling the discus along the ground so that it followed slightly behind him.

Nanu went hurtling over the crossbar and, as he hit the ground, he grabbed the rolling discus and headed for the thrower's circle. He made his toss and it was a beauty.

As the discus soared heavenward, I drove up in the golf cart.

"Get in, kid."

Nanu jumped in and off we roared.

"The 440's about to start," I told him, "but we still have a chance. Get ready now. First the long jump and then the 440. Think you can make it?"

"Nanu do his best," said the boy.

"Okay — get going."

Nanu leaped out of the cart and started down the long-jump runway.

The gun sounded for the start of the 440, and it could just as well have been aimed at Nanu. He hadn't even completed the long jump, and the 440 was underway.

Nanu did his great leap, landed, and ran out of the pit. Meanwhile, I had jumped out of the cart and linked arms with Milo. He linked his with Nanu. Together we formed a "whip" and sent Nanu across the 440 starting line and down the track.

Milo and I watched him race down the field. The pace was starting to wear on him. He stumbled and nearly fell.

"He'll never make it," said Milo. "He's just too tired."

Then, up in the grandstand, an enormous man in a raccoon coat and ten gallon hat stood up and let out a terrible growl. I suddenly realized that was no man — it was the kid's tiger.

The sound of Harri's roar seemed to provide the needed stimulus. Because Nanu produced a fresh burst of speed that brought him neck-and-neck with the leader.

The kid matched him stride for stride right up to the finish line, and then, with a final effort, he passed him and broke the tape — the winner.

The stands went wild.

Nanu had broken the standing record in every event in the NCAA — the pole vault, the high jump, the long jump, the 440, the 880, the javelin throw, the shotput, and the discus throw!

And as if that wasn't enough joy to cheer this callous coaching heart, I saw two things that made me feel even happier.

The first thing was Gazenga, standing soaking wet at the arena entrance, cheering wildly for his godson's victory.

Harri and Jane watch Nanu closely as fans shout encouragement to the fabulous jungle boy.

And the second thing was Leopold, leaping over the hurdles, racing around the track, pursued by the tiger.

CHAPTER FOURTEEN

Some people say that winning isn't everything.

I agree with them.

Winning *isn't* everything.

It's the *only* thing.

I was reflecting on this the following morning, as Milo, Nanu, Jane, and I stood beside our luggage on the runway, ready to board the plane that would take us back to Merrivale.

Everything coming up roses for Archer at last.

"Okay, let's get aboard," I said.

"Wait a minute, Coach," said the kid. "We have something to tell you."

"Won't it keep till we get on the plane?"

"We're not getting on the plane," said Nanu.

"You're what??"

On their way to Zambia, Nanu and Jane bid Archer fare-well at the airport. Milo watches with his usual dubious expression.

"Nanu going back to jungle."

"Jane — talk to him!" I said.

"I'm going with him, Coach."

I turned on the kid.

"But I thought you wanted to be the world's greatest athlete."

"No, that's what *you* wanted. Nanu want to go home to be with his people."

I looked from the kid to the girl. Two very determined expressions.

"Okay, if that's what you want, Nanu, I'm not going to try to talk you out of it."

"No — *try* to talk him out of it," moaned Milo.

"No, Milo. If that's what the boy wants, I won't stop him." I turned to Nanu and started backing away. "I just hope that someday, somehow, somewhere, you'll give a thought to your old coach. And remember the things I taught you — "

I continued backing and talking.

"To fight hard — play to win — and never — "

Suddenly the kid dived at me and brought me down with a flying tackle. It seems I had nearly backed into a spinning propeller.

Nanu helped me to my feet.

"Good Lord," I said. "You saved my life!" I turned to Milo. "Did you see that, Milo? This boy saved my life."

"I saw it, Coach — he saved your life, all right."

"Oh, no!" said the kid. "I did it again."

I dusted off my clothes.

"Okay, we've got a plane to catch."

I picked up the luggage and started briskly toward our plane, with Nanu and the others behind me.

"Once we get back," I said, "we've got a lot to do. There's spring training, and the Olympics are coming up — "

I looked over my shoulder and saw the most crestfallen expression ever to darken a young face. I stopped and put down the luggage.

"You really want to go home, don't you, kid?"

Nanu nodded. I looked from the boy to Jane, and back to the boy again. I handed him the suitcase.

"Go on — get out of here. Kids like you are a dime a dozen."

Jane kissed me on the cheek.

"Take good care of him," I said, having trouble with my voice.

I managed a smile for the boy's sake.'

"It's kind of tough saying good-bye to the world's greatest athlete," I said.

"It's kind of tough saying good-bye to the world's greatest coach," said Nanu.

That was the last I saw of him.

Oh, I did catch one more glimpse as he was being mobbed by reporters at the ramp.

He and Jane were about to board a plane that linked with Zambian Airlines to take him home. The reporters had a dozen questions. They always do.

Gazenga was about to board with them. He saw me looking on, with my jaw dragging, and put a hand on my shoulder.

"You are doing a fine thing, Mr. Archer, to let the boy go. It is the way of his heart."

"I guess you're right," I conceded.

"I knew Nanu would come back," said Gazenga. "He will always be a simple country boy at heart."

"Don't be too sure," I said.

Over by the ramp I could hear one of the reporter's questions.

"Nanu — is it true you're returning to Zambia?"

"That is so," said the kid.

"But why?"

Nanu looked from one reporter to the other, adjusted the knot on the reporter's tie, and spoke.

"Fellas — let me tell you a little story — Picture a young boy growing up in the jungle — "

I started walking. Fast.

Milo was struggling to keep up.

"Where are you going, Coach? Our plane is *that* way — "

"I'm not going back," I said. "There's nothing for me at Merrivale."

"But where'll you go, Coach?"

"I don't know. I just want to get as far away from athletics as possible."

CHAPTER FIFTEEN

Sitting in our bamboo chairs, leaning against a hut near the Great Wall of China, I had a wonderful sense of freedom.

"Boy, when you get away, you really get away," said Milo.

"This is the life," I said. "No competition — no pressure — no problems — just free as a bird. This is what I've always wanted."

And I meant it.

I was through with sports. The exultant discoveries and then the numbing sense of loss. The winning teams and then the plunge to defeat.

Not for me. I'd had it.

But my thoughts were interrupted by the sight of something racing across the horizon.

It was a Mongolian pony.

"Now that's what I call fast," I said.

"Not as fast as Chin Yang," said an old Chinese man.

"What's a Chin Yang?" I asked.

For an answer, he pointed.

He pointed to a Chinese boy who was streaking across the plain, gaining on the pony, and then passing it.

"Chin Yang," said the old man.

Milo and I exchanged glances.

Then we jumped to our feet and raced after the kid.

"Wait — " I shouted. "My name is Archer — I'm a coach — "